DANGER AFTER DARK

Look for these books in the
Clue™ series:

#1 WHO KILLED MR. BODDY?
#2 THE *SECRET* SECRET PASSAGE
#3 THE CASE OF THE INVISIBLE CAT
#4 MYSTERY AT THE MASKED BALL
#5 MIDNIGHT PHONE CALLS
#6 BOOBY-TRAPPED!
#7 THE PICTURE-PERFECT CRIME
#8 THE CLUE IN THE SHADOWS
#9 MYSTERY IN THE MOONLIGHT
#10 THE SCREAMING SKELETON
#11 DEATH BY CANDLELIGHT
#12 THE HAUNTED GARGOYLE
#13 THE MUMMY'S REVENGE
#14 THE DANGEROUS DIAMOND
#15 THE VANISHING VAMPIRE
#16 DANGER AFTER DARK

DANGER AFTER DARK

Book created by A. E. Parker

Written by Dona Smith

Based on characters from the Parker Brothers® game

A Creative Media Applications Production

SCHOLASTIC INC.
New York Toronto London Auckland Sydney

Special thanks to: Susan Nash, Laura Millhollin, Maureen Taxter, Jean Feiwel, Ellie Berger, Craig Walker, Greg Holch, Kim Williams, Dona Smith, Nancy Smith, Veronica Ambrose, David Tommasino, Jennifer Presant, and Elizabeth Parisi.

ISBN 0-590-13743-3

12 11 10 9 8 7 6 5 4 3   7 8 9/9 0 1 2/0

Printed in the U.S.A.   40

First Scholastic printing, April 1997

For Karen

Contents

Allow Me to Introduce Myself . . .   1
1. Nervous Habits   4
2. The Million-Dollar Dolly   12
3. Riding Around   17
4. Who's Who?   24
5. Sundae School   31
6. Money May I?   37
7. Burning the Candle at Both Ends   43
8. A Little Horse   49
9. A Sour Note   55
10. Danger After Dark   61

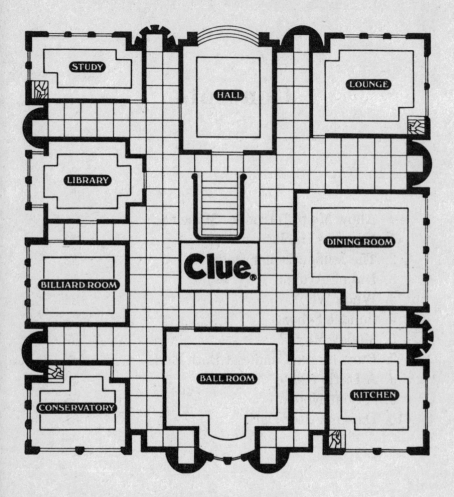

Allow Me to Introduce Myself . . .

MY NAME IS REGINALD BODDY, AND I'M happy to be your host for a long weekend of fun, frolic, and — er — fear. I've invited a few other guests I'm sure you'll adore. Live it up — while you still can.

You see, my cute and crazy crew of friends is a bit inclined to murder. But they're so much fun they're to die for! I learned *that* during their last visit, when Mr. Green tried to murder me with the Rope. But the joke was on him!

Poor Mr. Green was afraid that a vampire was loose in the mansion. He strung garlic around his neck for protection. I wasn't dead — I had merely fainted from the smell of the garlic fumes.

Of course, there really was no vampire in the mansion at all. It was only my cousin, Bitsy Boddy, dressed up as a vampire in order to play a prank. I must tell him "fang you" for providing everyone with a few laughs.

1

Oh, pardon me for *coffin*, it's just a tickle in my throat. Anyway, would you be kind enough to do me a favor and keep an eye on my guests this weekend? I don't want things to get bloody. There's too much at stake.

You only have six suspects to worry about. (I myself will never be a, I assure you, suspect.) The six suspects are:

Mrs. White: My loyal maid will sweep you off your feet. Unfortunately, you might not get up again.

Professor Plum: The man has quite a brain. Too bad he's so forgetful that he can't remember where he put it.

Mr. Green: If someone has what he wants, he gets *green* with envy. He soon takes steps — big ones — to take it from that person.

Miss Scarlet: She is lovely enough to be a model — a model criminal, that is. But watch out for those long, red nails — you may get scratched.

Colonel Mustard: This dynamic dueler will duel at the drop of a hat. Make sure you keep yours on your head!

Mrs. Peacock: The lady proves that there are manners among thieves. She is never rude, even when lying, cheating, and stealing.

To help you keep track of criminals and crimes,

I'll provide a list of rooms, suspects, and weapons at the end of each chapter. Good luck — you'll need it! Ha! Ha!

Now come along with me, and let the games begin!

1.
Nervous Habits

"**H**ELP!" CRIED MISS SCARLET. "I CAN'T stand that awful noise one moment longer!" She put her hands over her ears.

Clickety clackety clackety clickety clackety click. Mr. Green's teeth clicked together so loudly that they sounded like a freight train rolling down the track.

"Stop those teeth from chattering or I'll challenge you to a duel!" roared Colonel Mustard, waving the Candlestick threateningly. He tugged on his right ear, then his left.

Poor Mr. Green tried, but he couldn't help it. Like Colonel Mustard's ear-tugging, it was a nervous habit. All of the guests had developed a couple of them. You see, they were all obsessed with stealing a new treasure of Mr. Boddy's. It was a valuable original manuscript, the true confessions of that notorious art thief, Leonardo da Snitchy. They didn't know where in the mansion it was hidden, and it was making them all terribly nervous.

"Those chattering teeth sound *awful*," said Miss Scarlet, pointing at Mr. Green with the Lead Pipe.

4

It's a worse nervous habit than anyone else's, she thought. She tapped her right foot and then couldn't resist scratching her nose.

Mr. Green stopped his teeth from chattering long enough to point the Revolver at her and say, "It's better than listening to any chatter of yours. Though I must admit listening to your chatter is better than hearing someone sneeze time after time." He whistled softly. It was another habit he couldn't stop.

"Who put the tea kettle on?" asked another guest who was holding the Wrench. Then she realized it wasn't a kettle whistling — it was only Mr. Green. "Excuse me!" she said. "To see you all being so rude just wrenches my heart." She tapped her left foot and sneezed.

"They have been making some very cutting remarks," the guest with the Knife agreed. He hiccuped and his knees knocked together.

"Are you knock-kneed?" asked a female guest who hadn't spoken before. She was nervously twisting the Rope in her fingers.

The guest she had just spoken to was very forgetful, and had forgotten that his knees were knocking. "My knees knock, but I'm not knock-kneed," he answered her.

"I see," said the guest with the Rope. Her left eye twitched.

"Let's *twitch* again, like we did last summer," said Miss Scarlet with a smirk, as she looked at the guest with the Rope. Then she gave an exaggerated yawn. "Oh, dear, I'm so tired I must take a nap. I'm sure I'll sleep like a baby."

"I'm tired, too," said Colonel Mustard. "I bet I'll sleep like a log."

The other guests said they were also sleepy. Soon they all went to their rooms to take naps.

Of course, they were only pretending to be tired. They were all planning to sneak out of their rooms and search for the manuscript.

The first guest to leave her room headed toward the Kitchen. She thought Mr. Boddy might have hidden the manuscript in a cupboard.

A moment later, another guest got the same idea. They ran into each other in the Kitchen. "I was just trying to get this container of cocoa open," said the first guest, who was scratching her nose and tapping her right foot. She pretended to attempt to pry off the lid with her weapon.

"You'll find this much more useful," said the other guest, whose eye was twitching. "Wrap it around the lid and twist it off." The two guests exchanged weapons. Instead of having cocoa, the two guests made excuses for leaving the room and parted company.

Meanwhile . . .

Meanwhile, another guest was trying to pry open a cabinet in the Lounge. "I'll bet it's hidden in

6

here," he said. He hiccuped and his knees knocked together.

"Why not use this Wrench to wrench the cabinet open?" another guest said primly. But instead of giving him the Wrench, she bonked him on the head with it and stole his weapon. "Your nervous habits are the worst of all," she said. Then she sneezed.

At the same time . . .

At the same time, two other guests ran into each other in the Study. "I've always admired the weapon you have there," said a guest who was tugging at his right ear.

"I've always admired yours," said the other guest. Then he whistled softly.

The two guests exchanged weapons. "I have to be going," they both said at the same time. They bid each other farewell and left the room.

For a while, the mansion was quiet. Then, as if a signal had been given, all of the guests stirred from their rooms at the same time and went on the prowl.

In the Hall, one guest caught another one looking for the manuscript. The guest with the Revolver attacked the guest with the Lead Pipe. A struggle ensued, and the guest with the Lead Pipe won. She giggled as she ran from the room, so delighted that she momentarily lost all of her nervous habits.

She was *so* delighted, in fact, that she forgot that Mr. Boddy had warned them about running on the newly waxed floors. She slid halfway across the mansion and then slid through the open door to the cellar. The door slammed behind her.

Two other guests were in the Library and saw her slide into the cellar. I guess she's spending the night "down under," one guest said. The other guest laughed. Then they both saw Leonardo da Snitchy's manuscript on a bookshelf at the same time. Each guest lunged for it.

"Not so fast," cried a third guest who was entering the room. She attacked one of the guests, and grabbed the guest's weapon as the guest fell to the floor. Then she turned on the other guest, who was holding the manuscript.

"I don't hate your nervous habits as much as she did," she said, pointing to the guest on the floor. "But I'm a close second." Then she attacked the guest with a blunt instrument and ran off with the manuscript.

WHO STOLE THE MANUSCRIPT?

No!

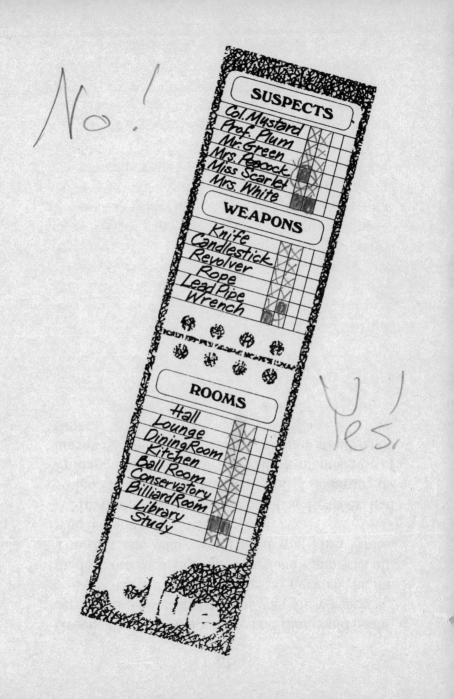

Yes!

Green. The only weapon she had that could be described as a blunt instrument was the Wrench.

As it turned out, the guests' nervous habits made them so shaky that everyone's aim was off. The only one who was bruised was Mrs. White, who fell down the stairs.

Mr. Boddy discovered that Mrs. Peacock had stolen the true confessions of Leonardo da Snitchy, and forced her to write a manuscript of her own. She had to write "I will not steal" 5,000 times.

10

SOLUTION

MRS. PEACOCK in the LIBRARY with the WRENCH

By noting each of the guests' nervous habits, we know who started off with which weapon. Mr. Green's teeth chattered and he whistled. He had the Revolver. Colonel Mustard, who tugged his ears, had the Candlestick. Miss Scarlet, who tapped her right foot and scratched her nose, had the Lead Pipe. The guest who thought the others were rude, and who had the Wrench, was Mrs. Peacock. She tapped her left foot and sneezed. The forgetful guest who hiccuped and had knocking knees was Professor Plum with the Knife. By process of elimination, we can figure out that the twitchy-eyed, finger-twisting guest with the Rope was Mrs. White.

Later on in the story, Mrs. White ended up with the Lead Pipe, Miss Scarlet had the Rope, Colonel Mustard had the Revolver, Mr. Green had the Candlestick, and Mrs. Peacock had the Wrench and the Knife.

Mrs. Peacock attacked Professor Plum and said that she hated his nervous habits most of all. Mrs. White attacked Colonel Mustard in the Hall and then fell into the cellar. Later, in the Library, Mrs. Peacock attacked Miss Scarlet, who hated Mr. Green's habits worst of all. She then attacked Mr.

2.
The Million-Dollar Dolly

MR. BODDY INVITED HIS GUESTS TO view his latest treasure, a valuable doll figurine. He had it on display on a table in the Study.

"Is that supposed to be Dolley Madison?" asked Mr. Green.

"No, the dolly isn't Dolley. It's my new doll," said Mr. Boddy.

The guests all looked at the doll, which had eyes made of sapphires and hair of real gold.

"I've been thinking of getting all dolled up myself," said Miss Scarlet, jealous that the doll was getting so much attention.

"You're always thinking about getting dolled up," said Mrs. White sourly.

"Be a doll and keep quiet, please, Mrs. White," said Mr. Boddy. He explained that the doll was quite valuable.

"Well, don't play games with us, Boddy," said Colonel Mustard. "Tell us how many dollars it's worth."

Mr. Boddy told them it was worth at least a million dollars.

The Colonel let out a low whistle. "It's a dilly of a dolly, isn't it?" he said.

Then Professor Plum spoke up. "Is that the kind of doll ventriloquists use? I've been struggling to remember what they are called."

"You mean a dummy, and you should speak for yourself," said Mrs. White with a sneer.

"I'd like to get a doll," said Mr. Green. "But what I really want is a special puppet, like a marionette. Do you know where I could purchase one, Mr. Boddy?"

"The best ones are hard to find, but I'll try and pull some strings," Mr. Boddy told him.

Then the guests pretended to be concerned about where the doll should be displayed. Of course, they were really all plotting to steal it.

"I think it belongs in the Library," said a guest, gesturing toward the Library with the Wrench that she held in her red-fingernailed hand.

"I disagree," said Colonel Mustard, pounding the Candlestick on the table for emphasis. "I think the dolly belongs in my dolly house."

"You have a dollhouse? Ha! Ha!" hooted Mr. Green.

Colonel Mustard challenged Mr. Green to a duel.

Mr. Boddy put a stop to it, saying, "Don't even toy with the idea of dueling now, gentlemen. And don't toy with taking my doll to your dolly house, either, Colonel Mustard."

"Well, I think the doll belongs in the Dining

Room," said Mr. Green, pointing toward the Dining Room with his weapon.

"I think the doll belongs in the Hall," said Mrs. White. She tried to gesture toward the Hall with her weapon, but it was impossible because it hung limply in her hands. She changed weapons with a guest who thought it was not polite to point. Then she pointed toward the Hall with the Lead Pipe.

Professor Plum stroked his chin thoughtfully. "I think it belongs in there," he said, using his weapon to point to a room diagonally across from the Study. All of the guests scoffed at him.

"Never mind," said Mr. Boddy. "The doll stays right where it is." He sat down and began reading a book by the famous author Roald *Doll.*

As soon as Mr. Boddy was absorbed in his book, the guest who said the doll belonged in the Kitchen went into action. When no one was looking, he grabbed the doll and ran from the Study. He soon forgot why he was running, however, and why he was holding a doll.

While he was trying to remember, another guest attacked him with the Revolver and seized the doll. "I said it belonged in the Dining Room, but it really belongs in *my* room," he chuckled.

"Hand it over," said a guest who snuck up behind him and attacked him with his weapon. No sooner did the guest get his hands on the doll when another guest surprised him.

"It wasn't polite to suggest that the doll belonged somewhere other than a room in Mr. Boddy's mansion," said the guest before attacking him and taking the doll. She took the doll to the room where the guest with the Revolver had suggested it be displayed. She intended to hide out and form a plan to get the doll out of the mansion.

While planning, the guest got hungry and decided to wander into the Kitchen and make herself a snack. "Perhaps I'll whip up some chili squares with whipped cream," she whispered, rubbing her hands together in anticipation.

When she was gone, another guest spied the doll and took it. She ran to the room where she had suggested the doll be displayed. She intended to wait there until it was safe to take the doll from the mansion. *I've never been a waiter, but I do know how to wait,* thought the guest, with visions of dollar signs in her head.

While the guest was waiting for the right moment, the guest with the Lead Pipe snuck in, attacked her, and grabbed the doll. Just then Mr. Boddy came charging in and caught the guest red-handed.

WHO WAS THE LAST TO STEAL THE DOLL? WHERE AND WITH WHAT WEAPON?

SOLUTION

MRS. WHITE in the LIBRARY with the LEAD PIPE

By paying careful attention at the beginning of the story, we know that Miss Scarlet with the Wrench says the doll belongs in the Library; Colonel Mustard with the Candlestick wants the doll in his dollhouse; Mr. Green says the doll belongs in the Dining Room. By process of elimination, we soon discover that Mr. Green later attacked Professor Plum with the Revolver; Mrs. White said the doll belonged in the Hall, and couldn't gesture with the Rope, so she traded weapons with the polite Mrs. Peacock. Then Mrs. White had the Lead Pipe and Mrs. Peacock had the Rope. Forgetful Professor Plum had the Knife. By keeping careful account of who attacked whom, we know that Miss Scarlet stole the doll when Mrs. Peacock left it in the Dining Room. Then she took it to the Library, where Mrs. White attacked her with the Lead Pipe.

Mrs. White wasn't the only one to get into trouble with Mr. Boddy that day. Mr. Boddy had deliberately kept from his guests the fact that the doll could talk, and was also a tattletale. The doll told him that every one of the guests had tried to steal her. He put them all to work making doll clothes.

3.
Riding Around

THE GUESTS WERE ALL PACING REST-lessly in the Conservatory. It was a beautiful day and they couldn't decide what to do.

"I think a game of croquet would be smashing," said Mrs. Peacock. She smoothed her ankle-length dress and pulled her collar up so high that it covered her face nearly to the eyes.

"It would be smashing. That's the problem," said Mr. Green with a shake of his head. "The last time we played croquet everyone tried to knock each other in the head with the mallets. We all had more lumps than a bowl of sugar cubes."

"I know!" Miss Scarlet said eagerly. "We can have a garden party, and I can be the queen. Just leaf everything to me."

"I'm not sure that's the best idea," Colonel Mustard hedged. "I think we're all too bushed for a party. I'd rather just go swimming."

"I have a much better idea," insisted Mrs. White. "Let's have a bake-off. You'll all bake something, and I'll sample your creations and judge which one is best."

17

The other guests roared with laughter. They thought that was the most half-baked idea yet. But they didn't like the last two suggestions either. Mr. Green wanted to have a dance, and Professor Plum wanted to make macaroni animals.

Everyone started arguing about what to do. A war was about to erupt when Mr. Boddy walked in. He saved the day by announcing the opening of his new amusement park, Corny Island. Everyone was delighted and couldn't wait to go.

"My very favorite ride at an amusement park is the roller coaster, and my favorite snack is cotton candy," said the guest who suggested the garden party.

"My favorite snack is peanuts, which I love to eat while riding my favorite ride, the Ferris wheel," said the guest who had wanted to make macaroni animals.

"Nuts to you, pea-brain," said the guest who suggested the bake-off. "My favorite ride is the merry-go-round, and my favorite snack is popcorn."

"My pop liked popcorn, but I prefer candy apples," said the guest who suggested the dance. "My favorite ride is the bumper cars."

"Take care that you don't get bumped off," said the remaining female guest, who had the same favorite ride as Mrs. White, and the same favorite snack as Miss Scarlet.

The remaining male guest had the same favorite ride as Professor Plum, and the same favorite snack as Mr. Green.

Soon the guests were at the amusement park, riding their favorite rides and eating their favorite snacks. After a while, they each got bored with riding the same ride over and over and decided to try something else.

The guest on the roller coaster took her favorite snack and tried Mrs. White's favorite ride.

The guest on the Ferris wheel who was eating peanuts decided to try Mr. Green's favorite ride.

The other guest on the Ferris wheel decided to try Mrs. Peacock's favorite snack and Miss Scarlet's favorite ride.

The guest whose favorite ride was bumper cars decided to try Professor Plum's favorite ride and Miss Scarlet's favorite snack.

The guest on the merry-go-round who was eating popcorn took the snack and went to try out Mr. Green's favorite ride.

The other guest on the merry-go-round decided to try Professor Plum's favorite snack and his favorite ride, as well.

After a while, the guests got bored with their snacks and started eyeing each others'. Everyone was sure that there was something better than what they had.

Miss Scarlet tried the snack Mrs. White was eating.

Colonel Mustard tried the snack Professor Plum was eating.

Professor Plum tried the snack Miss Scarlet was eating.

Mr. Green and Mrs. White tried the snack Mrs. Peacock was eating.

Mrs. Peacock switched back to her own original favorite.

The guests munched happily on their snacks, contented with the rides they had chosen. This didn't last long, however. Soon the guests grew bored with their rides once more.

Miss Scarlet switched with Mr. Green.

Professor Plum switched with Mrs. Peacock.

Colonel Mustard switched with Mrs. White.

After a few more minutes, Mr. Boddy, who was dizzy from having gotten lost in the Hall of Mirrors, announced that it was time to go home.

WHICH GUEST WAS ON WHICH RIDE? EATING WHAT SNACK?

5/6

√ Scarlet - ferris wheel - popcorn
√ Green - marry-go-round - peanuts
⊗ Plum - ferris wheel - ~~popcorn~~
√ Peacook - bumper cars - cotton candy
√ Mustard - bumper cars - peanuts
√ white - roller coster - penuts

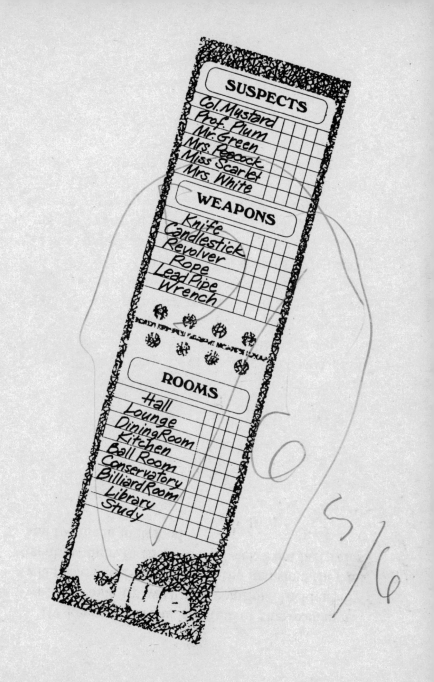

By keeping careful account of the exchanges, we can come up with the solution. Incidentally, when the guests got back to the mansion, they all went straight to their rooms, sick from fast rides and too much junk food.

SOLUTION

MISS SCARLET was on the Ferris wheel eating popcorn. MR. GREEN was on the merry-go-round eating peanuts. PROFESSOR PLUM was on the Ferris wheel eating cotton candy. MRS. PEACOCK was on the bumper cars eating cotton candy. COLONEL MUSTARD was on the bumper cars eating peanuts. MRS. WHITE was on the roller coaster eating peanuts.

By matching up the guests' initial activity suggestions with their favorite rides and snacks, we know that things started out this way:

Miss Scarlet was on the roller coaster eating cotton candy. Professor Plum was on the Ferris wheel eating peanuts. Mrs. White was on the merry-go-round eating popcorn. Mr. Green was on the bumper cars eating a candy apple. Mrs. Peacock was on the merry-go-round eating cotton candy. Colonel Mustard was on the Ferris wheel eating a candy apple.

4.
Who's Who?

PROFESSOR PLUM WAS THRILLED. HE had been working all day and night in the special laboratory Mr. Boddy had built for him, and he had concocted a miracle perfume. One whiff, and whoever smelled it developed a perfect memory. Or so he thought . . .

"His memory hasn't improved one bit," said Mr. Green, leaning back in his chair. The guests had gathered in the Lounge to discuss the problem with Professor Plum.

Mrs. Peacock brushed a speck of dust from the table in front of her, and began looking for more. "He's just as forgetful as ever," she said as she inspected. "In fact, I think his memory has gotten worse."

"I think so, too, and I've told him so," said Miss Scarlet, tapping her red nails on the arm of her chair.

"So have I," said Mr. Green. "He won't believe us. And he's acting strangely. I think smelling that perfume does more than make him more forgetful.

There are some weird side effects," he added, scratching his side.

It was true. Professor Plum's memory hadn't improved one bit, and after smelling the perfume, he'd forget what he was trying to improve. The other guests couldn't persuade him that he was wrong, either. He remained convinced that he had developed an amazing memory.

Unfortunately, instead of improving memory, the perfume did something else. It turned Professor Plum into a regular Dr. Chuckle and Mr. Snide. By day he went around laughing hysterically and skating down the halls of the mansion wearing a purple beanie. By night he turned nasty, making rude and sarcastic remarks to everyone. His memory got worse and worse. It got so bad, in fact, that he forgot who he was. He became firmly convinced that he was Mr. Green.

"What's the matter with you now? Why are you wearing that?" asked Mr. Green when he saw Professor Plum wearing one of his own expensive Giorgio Pastrami suits in lime green.

"Why shouldn't I be wearing it?" Plum answered. "I am Mr. Green."

"That's ridiculous. *I'm* Mr. Green," said Mr. Green. Then he burst out laughing. "I was only kidding. I'm Professor Plum. I guess I'm just not myself today."

Mr. Green thought it was true. It turned out

that the perfume's aroma had been wafting through the mansion, and it made *all* the guests forgetful.

"I challenge you to a duel!" another guest roared. "*I* am Professor Plum."

Both guests who thought they were Professor Plum hurried upstairs to change and came down wearing Plum's purple clothing. The outfit looked particularly silly on Mr. Green, who was much shorter than Plum and kept tripping over his pant legs.

"Highly improper and very rude," said a guest with long red nails who had become convinced that she was Mrs. Peacock. When she looked down at her red dress she shrieked with alarm. "This dress is scandalous!" she cried. She ran to put on a peacock blue dress with extra-long sleeves and an extra-high collar.

"I can't wait to get out of this dowdy blue frock," whispered another guest as she hurried to put on one of Miss Scarlet's clinging red dresses.

"I challenge me to a duel!" yelled the maid, when she saw what she was wearing. She raced upstairs to put on one of Colonel Mustard's yellow suits.

"I challenge you to a duel!" called the real Colonel Mustard, who had remembered who he was for a moment. "Who do you think you are?" Then Colonel Mustard forgot who he was again. His next words were, "Oh, dear me! How rude of me! I must mind my manners." He had assumed his second false identity. He ran to put on a high-necked dress.

"How rude!" muttered another guest in a high-necked dress as she watched him go. Then she stammered, "Why did I say that? I forgot." The guest shrieked, "Aaagh! Why am I wearing a dress?" The guest ran to change into a purple suit to go with her second false identity.

As the odor of perfume got stronger and stronger, things got more and more confusing. The guest who had assumed the identity of Colonel Mustard got hit in the head by a falling object while practicing dueling. The guest then assumed a second false identity — Mr. Green — and went to change into a green suit. As she did, she passed another guest who was racing to change from a green suit into a mustard yellow suit.

The real Mr. Green changed out of his purple suit and into a maid's outfit to go with his second false identity.

The guest in red decided to stay in that outfit — for the time being.

It didn't take long before every guest thought he or she was yet another guest. They kept changing clothes to go with their new identities.

The *real* Professor Plum exchanged false identities with the *real* Mrs. Peacock.

The *real* Colonel Mustard exchanged false identities with the *real* Mrs. White.

Then the *real* Mr. Green and the *real* Miss Scarlet exchanged false identities.

Mr. Boddy returned from an errand and noticed something was wrong immediately. He could tell that everyone thought he or she was someone else, and clarified the mix-up instantly.

WHO WAS WHO?

Plum - scarlet
Mustard - green
Green - plum
Scarlet - white
Peacok - Mustard
White - Peacock

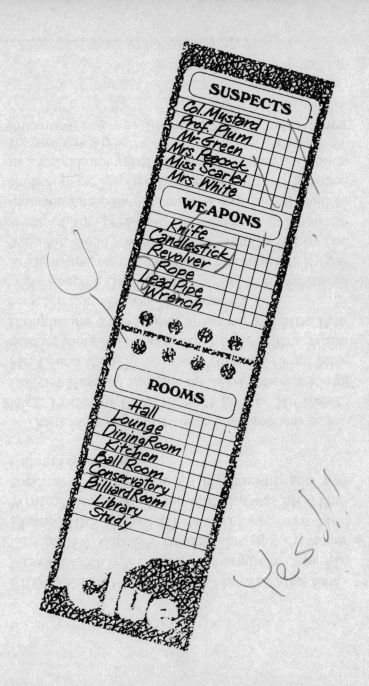

SOLUTION

PROFESSOR PLUM thought he was Miss Scarlet; COLONEL MUSTARD thought he was Mr. Green; MR. GREEN thought he was Professor Plum; MISS SCARLET thought she was Mrs. White; MRS. WHITE thought she was Mrs. Peacock; and MRS. PEACOCK thought she was Colonel Mustard.

The first false identity each assumed was as follows: Professor Plum thought he was Mr. Green; Colonel Mustard thought he was Professor Plum; Mr. Green thought he was Professor Plum; Miss Scarlet thought she was Mrs. Peacock; Mrs. White thought she was Colonel Mustard; and Mrs. Peacock thought she was Miss Scarlet.

By keeping track of the changes and exchanges in identities, we can figure out the solution. By the way, Mr. Boddy was strangely unaffected by the scent of the perfume. He removed it from the mansion immediately, and the guests returned to their senses. Mr. Boddy disposed of the fragrance in a neighbor's yard. The neighbors haven't been themselves since.

5.
Sundae School

It WAS A RAINY AFTERNOON, AND MR.
Boddy decided to liven things up by having a contest. Each guest was to try to create the most unusual ice-cream sundae ever.

"What for?" The disgruntled guests asked at once. No one was interested until Mr. Boddy gave them the scoop that the prize was a jade ice-cream cone.

"We all scream for ice cream!" the guests all shouted enthusiastically as they hurried to the Kitchen. There, they found six dishes of plain vanilla ice cream lined up on the counter.

"You are invited to add any assortment of toppings you wish," said Mr. Boddy. "Remember, the object is to create the most *unusual* sundae, not necessarily the best-tasting one."

"Too bad you can't compete. You might do well, since you have such bad taste," Miss Scarlet told Mrs. White.

"Well, your taste ought to be washed out of your mouth with soap," retorted Mrs. White.

"Ladies, ladies, please, no bickering," admonished Mr. Boddy. "I'm allowing my maid to compete. Now please get started making your sundaes." He placed the jade ice-cream cone on the Kitchen table.

The guests began pulling things out of the Kitchen cabinets. They didn't use traditional toppings such as chocolate syrup and whipped cream. They used things like beans, chili peppers, cheese, potato chips, sour cream, and onions.

Mrs. White started off her sundae with a spoonful of beans.

Miss Scarlet took tomatoes from the refrigerator, cut thick slices, and placed them on her sundae.

Mrs. Peacock chose parsley, while Mr. Green chose his favorite snack, ham.

Professor Plum pondered for quite a while before beginning with a dollop of sour cream.

Naturally, Colonel Mustard started with mustard.

When she thought no one was looking, Miss Scarlet took the jade cone from the kitchen table where Mr. Boddy had left it. Then she cheerfully added radishes to her sundae.

"Is that going to be called a Scarlet Sundae?" Mrs. White asked her.

"Mind your own business," Miss Scarlet snapped, annoyed at being distracted.

Mrs. White sneered at her, then added chili peppers to her sundae, followed by cheese.

While Miss Scarlet was distracted, Colonel Mustard grabbed the cone. He whistled happily as he added catsup to his sundae, then topped it with mayonnaise, followed by pickle relish.

"Your sundae is topped with condiments," Mr. Green remarked.

"There are no candy mints on it!" thundered Colonel Mustard.

"I didn't say *candy mints*, I said *condiments*," Mr. Green explained wearily. He hoped that Colonel Mustard wouldn't be tiresome and challenge him to a duel. Happily, he didn't.

While Colonel Mustard was in a snit, Mr. Green managed to steal the valuable cone. He held it behind his back while he added mayonnaise, then onions, then cheese, then potato chips to his sundae. "I call it a Sundae Picnic!" he said triumphantly as he admired his creation.

Professor Plum, sure that he was having a stroke of genius, sprinkled powdered hand soap on top of his sundae.

"Ugh!" said Mrs. Peacock. "What do you call that concoction?"

Professor Plum thought for a moment. "I'll call it my Cream of Washroom Sundae."

"Isn't there a Cream of Mushroom Sundae?" asked Miss Scarlet as she sprinkled chopped onions on her sundae.

"No, that's cream of mushroom *soup*," said Mrs. Peacock. While everyone else was looking at the

Cream of Washroom Sundae, she managed to sneak the cone away from Mr. Green. Then she added vinegar, followed by lettuce and then cucumber to her sundae. "I call it a Garden Sundae!" she announced.

Mrs. White finished off her sundae with a dollop of sour cream. "I call this my Chili Pepper Cheese Burrito Sundae," she said.

Miss Scarlet grabbed the vinegar and sprinkled some on her sundae. She grabbed the jade cone from Mrs. Peacock, as well.

Professor Plum astounded everyone by adding hand towels to his sundae to complete the washroom theme.

Miss Scarlet was admiring her creation, which she called a Salad Sundae, when the guest whose third topping was mayonnaise stole the cone from her. But he soon lost it to the guest who had followed a topping of cheese with one of sour cream.

That guest didn't hold on to the cone for long, for the guest whose first topping was sour cream managed to snatch it.

That guest soon had the cone stolen by the guest who had added onions followed by vinegar to a sundae.

No sooner did the guest congratulate herself on her cleverness than the guest who had followed a vinegar topping with lettuce managed to get it away from her.

She was about to slip the cone into her pocket

when the guest who had added onions followed by cheese grabbed it.

At that point, Mr. Boddy noticed the cone was missing.

WHO WAS THE LAST TO STEAL THE CONE?

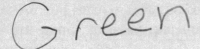

Green

Yes!

SOLUTION

MR. GREEN

The key is to pay careful attention to the order in which each guest added ingredients, which is as follows: Mrs. White: beans, chili peppers, cheese, sour cream. Miss Scarlet: tomatoes, radishes, onions, vinegar. Mrs. Peacock: parsley, vinegar, lettuce, cucumber. Colonel Mustard: mustard, catsup, mayonnaise, relish. Mr. Green: ham, mayonnaise, onions, cheese, potato chips. Professor Plum: sour cream, soap, hand towels. The only guest who added onions followed by cheese was Mr. Green.

Mr. Boddy insisted that unless Mr. Green confessed and turned over the cone, everyone would have to eat their own creations . . . so of course, he did.

6.
Money May I?

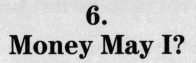

MR. BODDY SUMMONED HIS GUESTS TO his private playground. "We're going to play a game," he said. "It's called 'Money May I?' and the prize is lots of money. Here is how it works. I'll give you various commands such as 'Hop on one foot,' or 'Take three giant steps.' If I don't say 'Money says' first, you shouldn't follow the command. That is, unless you first ask, 'Money may I?' If I say 'Money says yes,' you *should* follow the command. If I say 'Not for my money,' don't do it or you'll be out. Get it?"

"Sure, I'm game," said Mr. Green.

"I'll take steps to win," said Miss Scarlet. "Giant steps."

"Well, then, let's hop to it," said Mr. Boddy, before anyone else could speak up. "Line up in alphabetical order from left to right. If Professor Plum has trouble remembering the alphabet, please help him."

"I'm always at the end of the line," grumbled the woman who took her place at the far right.

"I like being on the end," smirked the male

guest who took his place at the other end of the line.

The guests shuffled around, pushing and shoving. Somehow, they managed to line up.

When the guests had finally taken their places, the male guest who was next to the guest on the far left began muttering that he would rather be on the end.

"That is so rude, to want to change places!" huffed the guest who was second from the left — that is, next to the complaining guest.

"Mind your own business! You're always correcting other people's manners!" snapped the guest who was second from the right in a rare show of temper. "Let them do as they please," he added.

The two gentlemen at the left end of the line traded places. The two women at the other end of the line also traded places. Not wanting to feel left out, the guests who were second and third from the right also changed places.

The guests all glared at each other, sure they each had been cheated out of a better position.

The guest who was third from the left switched with the guest who was fourth from the right.

The guest who was third from the right switched with the guest who was fourth from the left.

The guests at either end switched.

"Stop moving about!" cried Mr. Boddy. "Let's

get the game started!" Knowing that money talks, he commanded, "Money says talk!"

The guests began talking, talking, talking, about anything that came to mind.

"Money says stop talking!" Mr. Boddy called out.

The guests fell silent. Then Mr. Boddy said, "Money says touch your nose and twirl around and around!"

Everyone twirled.

"Stop twirling!" Mr. Boddy said loudly. None of the guests stopped twirling except for the female guest next to the guest who was third from the left.

"Sorry, but you are out," said Mr. Boddy.

Complaining bitterly of unfair treatment, the guest took a seat on the sidelines and kept up an incessant whine.

"Oh, let her come back in the game and take my place," said the guest who had told Mrs. Peacock to mind her own business. "I'm tired of twirling. I'm getting dizzy and it is giving me a headache."

"You certainly are dizzy," the guests all said at once. Mr. Boddy shushed them. He let the guest he had thrown out come back into the game and take the place of the dizzy guest. Then he continued the game.

"Money says keep twirling, move to the right, and close up the line."

The guests did as they were told.

"Money says everyone stop twirling," Mr. Boddy commanded.

Everyone did.

"Money says bark like a dog!"

Everyone began howling.

"Money says hop on one foot!"

Everyone continued howling and began hopping on one foot.

"Laugh like a hyena!" commanded Mr. Boddy.

The guest who was second from the left spoke up and said, "Money may I?"

Mr. Boddy said the guest had to leave the game since he had stopped barking like a dog without being told to.

"But I had to, to ask 'Money may I?' That isn't fair!" the guest protested. Mr. Boddy waved him away from the playing area.

In an unusual show of friendship, the other guests protested. "After all, you said we could ask 'Money may I?'" said Miss Scarlet. "It should be allowed."

"If you don't let him back into the game, I'll challenge you to a duel!" Colonel Mustard said furiously.

The other guests stared at Mr. Boddy, waiting for his decision. Finally he relented. "I suppose my guests are right," he said after a moment. "You can come back into the game."

The guest came back, but instead of taking the

same place, he stood at the far right end of the line.

When Mr. Boddy wasn't looking, the guest who was third from the right switched places with the guest who was second from the left.

Mr. Boddy resumed the game. "Everyone clap your hands together like seal flippers!"

The guest who was third from the left did, and got thrown out of the game. Mr. Boddy had the other guests move to the right to close up the line.

"Money says flap your arms like a bird."

Everyone did, except the woman at the end of the line, who got sent out of the game.

The other guests kept flapping their "wings."

"Stop flapping!" Mr. Boddy called.

Only the woman in the center kept flapping.

WHO WON THE GAME?

White ?

Nor

41

42

SOLUTION

MRS. PEACOCK

By lining the guests up in alphabetical order from left to right, we know that we started with: Mr. Green, Colonel Mustard, Mrs. Peacock, Professor Plum, Miss Scarlet, and Mrs. White. This makes Colonel Mustard first from the left, Mrs. Peacock second from the left, and so on. By keeping track of everyone's position at each stage of the game, we know the three guests who were left were Mrs. White and Mr. Green on either side of Mrs. Peacock.

7.
Burning the Candle at Both Ends

MISS SCARLET BURST INTO THE lounge, where Colonel Mustard was reading. She looked particularly pleased with herself.

"You're looking particularly pleased with yourself, Miss Scarlet," remarked Colonel Mustard.

"Yes," she purred. "I've just been given a present. It's worth twelve thousand dollars." She pulled a candle encrusted with gold and diamonds from her purse. "It is a special kind of candle that will burn forever," she said dreamily.

"Where did you get it?" asked Colonel Mustard, tapping his fingers against the Wrench in his pocket and thinking of how he'd like to wrench the candle away from her.

"It was a gift from an old flame," said Miss Scarlet. "He ran off with a rattlesnake charmer, but has since seen the error of his ways. He hopes to rekindle our romance."

"Don't let that snake charmer rattle you," said Colonel Mustard. "I'm sure she can't hold a candle to you."

"Certainly not this one," said Miss Scarlet, admiring her treasure.

Another guest who stood outside the door clutching the Knife heard the whole conversation and tiptoed away quietly, plotting how to steal the candle.

"Perhaps you and this old flame of yours weren't the perfect match," said Colonel Mustard, eagerly eyeing the candle. Another guest on the way into the Study stopped and fingered the Candlestick in her pocket as she stopped to eavesdrop.

"Perhaps you're right about my old flame," she heard Miss Scarlet say. "He doesn't strike me as my perfect match anymore. I think he's lost some of his spark. But still, he gave me this very valuable candle."

And I've got the perfect candleholder, thought the guest who had overheard. She smiled as she left the door of the Lounge, plotting how to steal the candle.

Another guest holding the Lead Pipe confronted her in the Hall. "You'd better tell me why you've got that smirk on your face," she said, brandishing her weapon.

"Oh, all right," the other guest said grudgingly. "You're such a grouch. Miss Scarlet has just acquired a valuable candle worth lots of money. Satisfied?"

"Yes, I am," said the other guest, now wearing a

smirk of her own. She, too, was planning to steal the candle.

Back in the Lounge, Miss Scarlet said, "Maybe it wasn't very bright of me to tell you how valuable the candle is, Colonel Mustard."

"Nonsense!' he replied. "You can trust me."

"Well, don't tell the others," Miss Scarlet whispered. "I'd like to keep them in the dark about its value." She was glad she had brought the Rope with her. She got all choked up when she thought about the candle being stolen.

"I promise I won't tell anyone else about the candle," said Colonel Mustard.

Neither he nor Miss Scarlet knew that a guest had been hiding behind a chair the entire time, holding the Revolver.

Later that night . . .

Later that night, a guest crept toward Miss Scarlet's room holding the Lead Pipe.

"I never knew Miss Scarlet snored," she said to herself as she grabbed the candle.

She started to leave the room when she was surprised by the guest with the Revolver, who took the candle from her.

"The candle is all mine!" he whispered joyfully. He was halfway to his room when he looked at the object in his hand and was suddenly puzzled.

"What am I doing with a candle?" he asked himself as he scratched his head. "Aren't the electric lights working properly?"

"Why don't you let me take that off your hands before I give you a few *wax?*" asked a guest who was walking by and twirling the Wrench. The other guest handed over the object.

"What an idiot!" chuckled the guest with the Wrench as he walked away with the candle. He wasn't chuckling anymore when he was attacked in the Billiard Room by the guest with the Candlestick, who made off with the candle.

She had nearly made it back to her room when she was surprised by the guest with the Knife. They struggled, losing their own weapon and picking up the other guest's weapon in the scuffle. The guest who now had the Candlestick smiled to himself as he knocked out the other guest and took the candle. He could hardly believe he was fortunate enough to possess an object worth twelve thousand dollars.

WHO WAS THE LAST TO STEAL THE CANDLE?

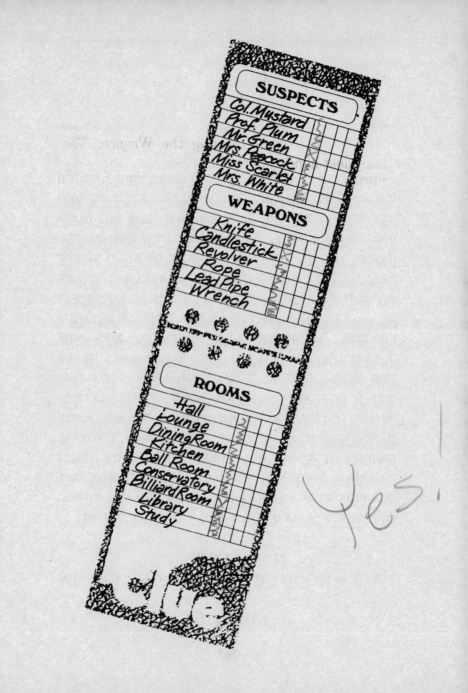

SOLUTION

MR. GREEN in the BILLIARD ROOM with the CANDLESTICK

The key is to remember which guests knew the candle was worth exactly twelve thousand dollars. The forgetful guest with the Revolver, Professor Plum, knew, but he gave the candle to Colonel Mustard, who had the Wrench. Colonel Mustard knew how much the candle was worth, but he was attacked by the guest with the Candlestick. The only remaining guest who knew the candle was worth twelve thousand dollars was Mr. Green, who took the candle after exchanging weapons with the female guest with the Candlestick. Mr. Green didn't keep the candle, though. He had gotten up very early, and he stayed up very late in order to steal the treasure. He fell asleep outside the door to his room. Miss Scarlet rose early the next morning and found him, and she took back her candle. When the other guests woke up, they didn't remember a thing.

8.
A Little Horse

IT WAS A BEAUTIFUL DAY ON THE Boddy Estate. Mr. Boddy was showing off his new stable and collection of magnificent new horses to his guests.

There were six horses, each a different color. There was a golden palomino, a spotted horse called a pinto, a dappled gray, a reddish bay horse, a reddish horse with lots of white "sprinkles" called a roan, and a chestnut brown horse.

"You are all welcome to choose a horse and go for a ride," Mr. Boddy announced.

"I'm the best rider so I should have first choice," said Mrs. White.

"You can't even ride in a car, though you might do all right on a broomstick," said Miss Scarlet.

"I'm the only one who knows how to be a proper rider," said a guest, choosing the bay horse. "Good manners are the most important thing in riding."

"*Neigh, neigh!*" protested the man who chose the roan. "I can ride rings around you. In fact, I'll bet I'd win a race against you."

"Ha! I mean, hay!" said a guest who was feeling

his oats. "You're far too unstable to be a good rider. Clearly I'm the best one here." He hopped on the pinto.

Another guest bridled at his remarks. "I challenge you to a duel!" said the guest who was about to mount the dappled gray.

"Take it easy, please," said Mr. Boddy. "Let's everyone have a nice ride. That's the most important thing, not competition."

"Perhaps I did put the cart before the horse," said the guest who had wanted to duel. He changed his mind about choosing his horse, and took the chestnut.

The last two guests fought over who would take the palomino and who would get the dappled gray, changing their minds again and again about which was the better horse. The other guests continued to fight about who was the best rider.

Mr. Boddy was getting a headache from it all. *I certainly managed to stirrup quite a mess*, he thought. *Now I'm saddled with a lot of angry guests.*

The arguing got louder and louder. All of the guests were demanding a race.

"That's the last straw!" Mr. Boddy finally screamed at the top of his lungs. "You can have your race. I'll even provide a surprise prize. Just stop arguing!"

The remaining guests quickly got seated on

horses. Mr. Boddy had everyone line up on the track behind the starting line.

"On your mark, get set, go!" he called. The horses leaped forward and began galloping down the track.

Soon the palomino and the pinto were neck and neck, followed by the chestnut, the dappled gray, and then the roan. The bay horse trailed behind.

"Come on, you! It's rude to be so far behind!" the rider of the bay horse muttered. She took the Wrench out of her pocket and prepared to chuck it at the rider two horses ahead of her.

The guest on the dappled gray happened to turn and catch her as she was about to hurl the weapon. "Hee-haw!" she cried, swinging the Rope like a lasso and pulling the guest off the bay horse. "*Hay*, you!" she cried as the guest went flying into the air. "*Bale* out of the race."

The riderless bay horse cantered into the meadow and began eating grass. The rider on the dappled gray horse was very happy, and even happier when her horse surged ahead of the chestnut.

Meanwhile . . .

Meanwhile, the guest on the pinto and the guest on the palomino were desperately trying to outdo each other.

"You're not going to ruin my shot at winning,"

said the rider on the pinto. He took out the Revolver and aimed it at the rider on the palomino.

"Sorry, I'll have to cut you out of the race," said the other rider. She threw the Knife like a boomerang and cut the pinto's reins. She caught the handle of her weapon as it spun back to her.

The pinto's startled rider had no reins to hold on to. Matters got worse when the Revolver went off, causing the pinto to rear up on its hind legs and then buck like a bronco.

"That ought to rein you in!" chuckled the guest on the palomino. She clutched the reins firmly in her red-nailed hands. "Now eat my dust!" she said as she bounded forward.

All of the other horses quickly passed the bucking bronco.

"I've got to get the lead out!" fretted the guest on the roan. "It must be this Lead Pipe in my pocket that's slowing me down."

He pulled the Lead Pipe out of his pocket and threw it away. Immediately, his horse surged ahead. Soon he was neck and neck with the chestnut.

The rider of the chestnut pulled the Candlestick out of his pocket. "I'll challenge you to a duel if you try to pass me," he said, preparing to fight.

He needn't have bothered. "Why are we going so fast?" the guest on the roan asked himself suddenly. Then he slowed his horse to a walk and went off to smell the roses.

Soon the horses were coming down the home-stretch. "Hee-haw!" cried the rider on the horse in second place. For the second time she swung the Rope like a lasso. She caught the rider of the horse in front of her and sent her flying into the air to land beside the track with a thud. "Quit stalling!" she laughed as she passed the rider on the ground. Now that she was in the lead, she felt sure to win.

The rider on the chestnut horse urged his horse ahead, but couldn't catch her.

"The race is mine!" cheered the rider on the lead horse. But she spoke too soon. In a stunning feat of horsemanship and acrobatics, the rider on the horse trailing behind the other two somersaulted into the air, vaulting over the horse in front of him and landing on the lead horse just behind the rider. "Get off, or you've had it," he said, pointing his weapon at her.

She had enough horse sense to do as he said. He then rode the horse across the finish line to win the race.

WHO WON? ON WHICH HORSE? WITH WHICH WEAPON?

Green / gray / rev.

yes!!!

SOLUTION

MR. GREEN on the dappled gray with the REVOLVER

We can be sure that the lady who thought manners were the most important thing in riding was Mrs. Peacock, who chose the bay horse. Later we found out that she had the Wrench. The gentleman who wanted to duel with the Candlestick was Colonel Mustard, who chose the chestnut horse. The lady with the red nails on the palomino with the Knife was Miss Scarlet, so the lady on the dappled gray with the Rope was Mrs. White. The forgetful fellow who threw away the Lead Pipe must have been Professor Plum. By process of elimination we know that the guest on the pinto with the Revolver was Mr. Green. He vaulted on to Mrs. White's dappled gray, forced her off, and won the race.

The guests, who were all a little hoarse from arguing, weren't too happy with their surprise prizes. Mr. Boddy made them all muck out the stalls.

9.
A Sour Note

THE GUESTS WERE ALL HUDDLED IN the Kitchen, shivering and complaining. The furnace was broken, and Mr. Boddy couldn't get anyone to repair it until the following day.

In the meantime, he had done the best that he could to make his guests comfortable. He had provided each one with a cozy down quilt. Colonel Mustard got a plaid one, Miss Scarlet got one with stripes, Mrs. Peacock's had ruffles, Mrs. White's had polka dots, and Mr. Green had a checkered one. Professor Plum was given a black velvet quilt, but he lost it immediately.

"Brrrr, why is it so cold?" Professor Plum asked for the umpteenth time that evening. The others had told him again and again that the furnace was broken, but he kept forgetting.

"The furnace is broken," said Mr. Green. "That's why the mansion is cold as ice."

"Maybe it broke because Mrs. White forgot to dust it," said Miss Scarlet.

Mrs. White, who was standing behind her, swatted her on the head with an icicle.

"Hey, I *thaw* that," said Colonel Mustard.

"Well, what are you going to *duel* about it?" asked Mrs. Peacock with a sneer. She was so cold that she was almost becoming rude. It was clear that Colonel Mustard was shivering too hard to duel.

The guests were so cold that they were getting nastier and nastier. Mr. Boddy could see that something had to be done, and fast, or they would all kill each other.

"To pass the time and take your minds off the cold, why don't you all play musical instruments?" Mr. Boddy suggested. He reminded everyone that there was a harp in the Hall, an organ in the Lounge, a guitar in the Dining Room, a piano in the Ball Room, a set of drums in the Conservatory, and a harmonica in the Billiard Room.

Then the trouble started. "I'm the only one with any musical talent," boasted Colonel Mustard. "I can play every one of those instruments like a virtuoso."

His remarks made the other guests seethe with rage. They were all nursing grudges against Colonel Mustard because he had been so arrogant and boastful lately. Besides, they were fed up with him for challenging everyone to a duel all the time.

"I don't believe you're so talented!" blurted the guest wrapped in the ruffled quilt. "I can play all of those instruments except the harmonica, and I don't think you can do any better. Take note that I don't think you are that sharp."

"Nor do I," agreed the guest huddled under the polka-dotted quilt. "I can play the drums, harp, and guitar beautifully, and I know you can't be more talented than I am."

The guest clutching the striped quilt said that she could play the harp, piano, and guitar, although it was rough on the nails. "Colonel Mustard, you can go jump off a *clef*," she said in conclusion.

"Ha! Flat chance of that!" said the guest wrapped in the checkered quilt. He told everyone that he was a whiz on drums and harmonica, though he couldn't play anything else. He glared at the smirking Colonel Mustard and *trebled* with anger. He vowed to make him change his tune.

Professor Plum swore that he was once able to play all of the instruments, but he had forgotten how. He now asserted that occasionally the knowledge would return to him in a flash, only to disappear again.

Everyone waltzed off to play an instrument. The guest in plaid went to the Lounge, the guest in checks went to the Conservatory, the guest in stripes went to the Hall, the guest in ruffles went to the Ball Room, and the guest in polka dots went to the Dining Room. Soon they were all making beautiful music. All except Professor Plum, that is, who couldn't remember how to play an instrument at the moment. He walked back and forth, trying to keep warm.

Then the guest who was playing the piano spotted the black velvet quilt in a corner of the room. Thinking it would be rude not to give it to its rightful owner, she threw it over her own quilt, pulled it up over her head, and went off in search of him.

By now Professor Plum was shivering so hard that his teeth were practically rattling out of his mouth. When he saw a guest with his own black velvet quilt wrapped around her shoulders, he flew into a rage. "I hate *all* quilt thieves," he said, making a blanket statement. He thumped the guest on the head with the Wrench, seized both quilts, and rolled the guest into a closet.

Professor Plum started to wrap himself in the black quilt, but decided he liked the other one better and threw it over his shoulders instead.

Just then, all the lights in the mansion went off.

"Aaaagggghhhh!" shrieked the guests. In a panic, they all ran to the staircase, losing their quilts in the process.

A moment later, the lights snapped back on again. Each freezing guest ran to find a quilt — any quilt. They all succeeded, though no one found the quilt they had before.

Most of the guests had tired of playing musical instruments, and decided to seek revenge against

Colonel Mustard instead. But one guest went off to the Ball Room and began playing the instrument there so brilliantly that everyone who passed complimented her.

"Thank you," she called sweetly in reply to each one who praised her.

About a quarter of an hour had gone by when a guest crept up behind another guest who was wrapped in the plaid quilt and playing guitar in the Dining Room. "Take that, Colonel Mustard!" she cried, firing the Revolver at him.

The guitar squealed horribly as the guest fell to the floor. The guest holding the Revolver realized she had made a terrible mistake. "You remembered how to play the guitar!" she cried.

WHO SHOT THE WRONG GUEST?

White shot Plum
Dinning Room
Rev.

Yes!

SOLUTION

MRS. WHITE in the DINING ROOM with the REVOLVER

Mrs. White thought she was attacking Colonel Mustard in the plaid quilt. However, we know that none of the guests were wrapped in their original quilts, so it had to be someone else.

With Mrs. Peacock eliminated, the only female who could play the piano was Miss Scarlet. The guilty guest was a female, so it had to be Mrs. White. Since Mr. Green couldn't play the guitar, Mrs. White must have attacked Professor Plum, who had suddenly remembered how.

None of the guests were seriously injured. Mr. Boddy knew them well enough to make sure the quilts were slashproof, crashproof, and bullet-proof.

10.
Danger After Dark

"THAT'S A LIE!" SNAPPED MRS. WHITE. She had been the target of the first nasty rumor to be spread during the long weekend at Mr. Boddy's mansion.

It all started when the guests were sitting around in the Lounge arguing about who Mr. Boddy liked best. Mrs. White proudly declared herself the favorite.

"You?" Miss Scarlet scoffed scornfully. "Highly unlikely, considering what Mr. Boddy told me about you." She smiled as she waited for everyone to ask what it was.

She didn't have to wait long. Barely a second had gone by when everyone demanded to know what Mr. Boddy had told Miss Scarlet about Mrs. White.

Smiling sweetly, she told the other guests that Mr. Boddy had confided to her that Mrs. White was a terrible housekeeper. "In fact, he said she graduated from the Trash Can Housekeeping School," she said, looking at Mrs. White with satisfaction.

The rumor took off. Soon everyone was talking about it and giggling at Mrs. White. Mrs. White was furious that Mr. Boddy would tell such a terrible lie, and that anyone else would believe it.

But everyone *didn't* believe it. Mr. Green told Mrs. White he knew it wasn't true because she was a fine housekeeper. Miss Scarlet knew she had started a rumor that was a lie. She just wanted to get back at Mrs. White for saying that her new handbag was tacky. She laughed every time she thought of how angry the rumor made Mrs. White.

Miss Scarlet wasn't laughing, however, when rumor number two got started, because it was about her. Someone said that Mr. Boddy thought her fashion sense was so bad that she didn't know the difference between stripes, polka dots, and plaids. Miss Scarlet was outraged since she was sure she knew the difference.

Miss Scarlet didn't know the rumor was started by a male guest who didn't believe it. He only started the rumor to get back at her for starting the false rumor about Mrs. White. The other guests believed it, though.

Now that a rumor had already been started about Miss Scarlet, Mrs. White didn't need to start one. She decided to start one about Colonel Mustard instead. One day, when the guests were sitting in the Conservatory, she got her chance. "Did I ever mention that Mr. Boddy told me Colonel Mustard couldn't duel his way out of a paper bag with a pair of scissors?" she asked. "He said he saw it with his own eyes."

Mrs. White was quite pleased with herself when she saw how angry she had made Colonel Mustard. At last she had gotten back at him for challenging everyone to a duel all the time.

Mrs. White thought the rumor was a lie, but it was actually only an exaggeration. No one else believed rumor number three either except — surprise — Colonel Mustard himself. He remembered the duel-your-way-out-of-a-paper-bag-with-scissors contest, and how he had failed miserably.

Even though Mr. Green didn't believe rumor number three, he teased Colonel Mustard so unmercifully that Colonel Mustard decided to start a rumor about him. That was rumor number four. "Mr. Boddy told me he thought Mr. Green was so boring that he'd rather watch paint dry than talk to him — pass it on," he whispered in a guest's ear one day. The guest passed it on, and soon everyone was talking about it.

Colonel Mustard thought Mr. Green had been boring lately, and started believing Mr. Boddy had said that. So did Mrs. Peacock, Professor Plum, and Mrs. White.

Mr. Green thought he was a fascinating fellow, as did Miss Scarlet, who thought all men were fascinating.

Mrs. Peacock thought that spreading rumors was rude — but one day she was feeling particularly mischievous and started rumor number five. "I hate gossip," she said primly, "but I must say that Mr. Boddy told me that Professor Plum is so forgetful that one winter he forgot the difference between earmuffs and shoes, and went out wearing his favorite loafers on his ears!" She chuckled and felt quite daring.

Indeed, it was true. Mr. Boddy *had* mentioned it to her. All the other guests knew how forgetful Professor Plum was, and believed it was true. Even Professor Plum thought it was probably true — though he had forgotten the incident.

Still, it irked Professor Plum to have everyone laughing at him, so he started rumor number six. "One thing I'll never forget," he said one day when the guests had gathered in the Lounge, "is that Mr. Boddy told me Mrs. Peacock's only course in manners was from Sparkey's Pet Obedience School."

Mrs. Peacock turned red with rage. From that day on, all of the guests began teasing her.

"Fetch!" Miss Scarlet would say when she walked past her.

"Sit!" Mrs. White would order her when everyone sat down to a meal.

The others joined in, telling her to "give me your paw," "heel," or "roll over." Actually, no one believed the rumor except Mrs. White and Miss Scarlet.

One evening after it had gotten dark, the guests

paced up and down in the mansion, boiling with fury at each other and at Mr. Boddy. However, the guest who only believed rumor number five went to the Library to read.

"You didn't believe any other rumors except the one about me," said the guest who snuck up behind him and bonked him on the head with the Candlestick.

Another guest who overheard the commotion snuck in. "He was right to believe the rumor about you," she said as she choked the guest with her Rope. "I only believed one other rumor myself."

Elsewhere, the guest who started the rumor about Mr. Green spotted the guest who had started the rumor about *him*. Mr. Green spent the evening chasing the guest all over the mansion, without success.

Meanwhile . . .

Meanwhile, another guest who believed rumor number four set off in search of Mr. Boddy. The guest found him in the Study.

"It doesn't matter who spread the rumors. They're really all your fault. You are the one who started them all, and now you're going to pay for it!" said the guest in a threatening voice.

"But I didn't start any rumors!" Mr. Boddy protested. He glanced at his watch and had a feeling that time was running out.

65

He was right. The guest didn't believe him. Moments later, there was a loud *bang!* as the guest's weapon went off. Mr. Boddy fell to the floor.

WHO KILLED MR. BODDY?
WHERE?
WITH WHICH WEAPON?

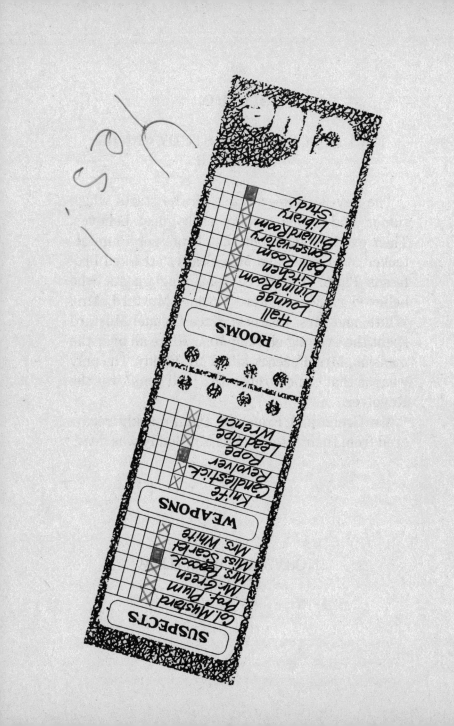

yes!

CLUE

SUSPECTS

Col. Mustard
Prof. Plum
Mr. Green
Mrs. Peacock
Miss Scarlet
Mrs. White

WEAPONS

Knife
Candlestick
Revolver
Rope
Lead Pipe
Wrench

ROOMS

Hall
Lounge
Dining Room
Kitchen
Ball Room
Conservatory
Billiard Room
Library
Study

SOLUTION

MRS. PEACOCK in the STUDY with the REVOLVER

The key is to keep track of who starts which rumor, and which rumors each guest believes. Then we can figure out that Professor Plum attacked Mr. Green, and Miss Scarlet attacked Professor Plum. The three remaining guests who believed rumor #4 were Colonel Mustard, Mrs. White, and Mrs. Peacock. Since Colonel Mustard spent the evening chasing Mrs. White all over the mansion, Mrs. Peacock killed Mr. Boddy. The only weapon that could go off with a loud *bang!* was the Revolver.

Mr. Green and Professor Plum quickly recovered from their attacks. But Mr. Boddy was dead.